BILLY'S MOUNTAIN

BY STEVE RICHARDSON

ILLUSTRATED BY HERB LEONHARD

ISNBN 0-9786422-0-1

To achieve the impossible, one must think the absurd;
to look where everyone else has looked, but to see
what no one else has seen.

– author unknown

Right smack in the middle of the state of Kansas, on a small farm near the town of Abilene, lived a boy named Billy. Billy's farm was surrounded with cornfields or wheat fields, depending on what his Dad planted each year. Billy had never been more than fifty miles from his farm, and he had never seen a mountain or a forest. In fact he had never seen much of anything but the flat prairie around his farm.

Billy had a favorite book that he looked at almost every day. It was a book about all the beautiful states in America. Billy liked looking at the pictures, especially the pictures of snow-capped mountains covered with green forests and giant waterfalls.

One day Billy had a wonderful idea. He would build a huge mountain right next to his farm! A mountain so big it would be covered with snow, green forests, and have beautiful waterfalls just like the pictures in his favorite book. Billy's mountain would have lakes on top, too, with real trout. It would have deer, elk, black bears and even beavers and moose; it would have all kinds of wildlife.

The next day Billy got all his friends to help him start building the huge mountain. Every day after school when Billy was done with his chores he would meet his buddies and they would get bucket loads of dirt and rocks and throw them in one spot. After several weeks, the hill was almost fifteen feet high and thirty feet wide. Billy began to feel discouraged that it was taking so long to build his mountain. He realized it would take years or even a lifetime to build the kind of mountain that he wanted to build, but he kept trying and so did all his friends.

After two months, Billy's Mountain was forty feet tall and one hundred feet wide. Billy was determined to keep going, but his friends were getting tired. They told Billy to "give up" building the mountain because it would never be nearly as big as Billy dreamed it could be. They even made fun of Billy for believing he could really build a snow-capped mountain in the middle of Kansas. "It's impossible," they all told him, "it was fun for a while Billy, but it's stupid to keep going!" The kids said.

Although Billy was hurt and somewhat discouraged by what his friends said, he wasn't the type to give up easily. That evening he sat on his forty-foot hill determined to find a way to finish his dream and build a real snow-capped mountain next to his farm!

Billy did come up with an idea that night, and the next day he put his idea into motion and invited a reporter for the Abilene Reflector-Chronicle, to see the 40-foot hill that he and his friends had built. Billy thought that perhaps if his mountain got some attention someone would help him build it.

Billy told the reporter, Ted McCoy (an old family friend) about his dream to build a snow-capped mountain next to his farm. The reporter was impressed the boys had worked so hard and found the story fascinating. The next day, Billy's story was printed on the front page of the Abilene newspaper, and the day after that it was in the national news.

Then something wonderful happened...

An old man named Jim, who was very wealthy and worked at the top of the tallest skyscraper in New York City read about Billy's dream. The old man was one of the richest and most powerful people in the world and was known for accomplishing anything he put his mind to. Old Man Jim had a saying: "If it's a difficult task, it will take some time to complete. If it's an impossible task, it will take a bit longer."

Billy and Jim were a lot alike in this respect. They were both persistent and would not give up on anything. Just like Billy, Jim thought it would be really neat to have a snow-capped mountain smack-dab in the middle of Kansas one of the flattest states in America. The old man liked the idea so much that he flew to Billy's farm that same day and told him he would help him build a magnificent mountain, even if it took every penny he had. You see, Old Man Jim grew up in Kansas, and when he was young he had big dreams just like Billy.

The very next day, Billy's dream started to become a reality as he watched thousands of construction workers, dump trucks, cranes, cement mixers and bulldozers driving past his little farmhouse and surrounding the 40-foot hill that he and his friends had built.

Even better, Billy was allowed to design the mountain and where he would put the streams, lakes, and waterfalls. He drew a picture of the mountain for Old Man Jim.

After several months, the mountain had grown from 40 feet to 500 feet tall as dozens of construction companies poured cement and dumped dirt, gravel and rocks. However, the mountain was far from being finished. It would take years to complete a mountain big enough to have trout streams and peaks covered with snow year round. Although progress was being made, Old Man Jim was not happy that it was taking so long. At the rate they were going, it would take 20 years to finish. Jim had to come up with a way to speed things up......but how?

After several days of thinking, Old Man Jim decided the only way to complete the mountain faster, was to have a railroad built from Kansas City to Billy's farm. Railroads could carry large equipment and the billions of tons of rock, concrete and dirt needed for the mountain much faster than by the dump trucks. They could also bring in the hundreds of thousands of small trees and the tons of grass and flower seed that would need to be planted after the mountain was finished. After several months, the train track was laid, and soon Billy saw hundreds of railroad cars speeding by his farm, filled with more dirt and materials for his mountain. Progress began to move much, much faster! It was very exciting for both Billy and Old Man Jim to see it all coming together and the mountain getting taller and taller.

Billy continued to stay involved with his mountain's construction. On weekends and after school he often helped Old Man Jim make important decisions and sometimes gave a hand to the construction workers.

After three years, the mountain was almost completely done and the workers were putting the finishing touches on the highest peaks. It was more than 15,000 feet tall, 20 miles long and about ten miles wide. Billy named the highest peak Mt. Eisenhower, after the famous president who grew up in Abilene, and he also named the largest lake after Wild Bill Hickok, the marshal of Abilene back in 1871.

Finally the mountain was done! It was enormous and towered
miles above Billy's farm, so high its tallest peak disappeared
above the clouds. It was one of the biggest mountains in the whole
country! The only problem was that there were no trees or grass
on it, it would take years for the trees to grow large and for Billy's
mountain to really look like the ones in his book. At first it was
kind of ugly and brown, but once the first winter came it was
covered with snow and looked beautiful!

In the spring, most of the snow began to melt, except on the highest peaks. The construction workers had spread grass and flower seeds over most of the mountain, and now grass and flowers started sprouting all over the slopes. They had also planted hundreds of thousands of small trees common to the Rocky Mountains. By April, the entire mountain was emerald green and covered with lush grass and flowers of every color. Its highest peaks were still capped with snow and in the canyons dozens of cascading streams began to flow.

The mountain was so tall it would catch the clouds that rolled by, and Billy noticed that for some reason it rained and snowed on the mountain much more than down on his farm. In the middle of the first summer, Billy and his dad hiked all the way to the top of the highest saddle where they looked out at the magnificent view to the east. They could see for hundreds of miles, and they were so high that the rolling clouds were close enough to touch.

As a teenager, Billy explored almost every inch of the magnificent mountain and knew every brook and lake. With each passing day, he began to notice more and more wild animals during his hikes. Many varieties of animals had already moved from the prairie onto the mountain; while other animals such as elk, moose, mountain lions, big-horned sheep and black bear were introduced from the Rocky Mountains. The creeks and lakes were also seeing new wildlife. Several of the bigger streams running off the range connected to nearby rivers, which allowed trout, salamanders and frogs to navigate up the creeks and into the heart of the mountain and its high-country lakes.

Billy loved how the mountain changed with each season.
His favorite time of year was fall when the trees around
his farm and on the mountain turned from bright green to
brilliant red and shimmering gold.

Winters on the mountain were harsh, but heavy snowfall often left the high country looking like an illustration in a book of fairy tales.

Spring always brought melting snow and bubbling brooks. The long, rainy days gave way to lush green slopes covered with wildflowers.

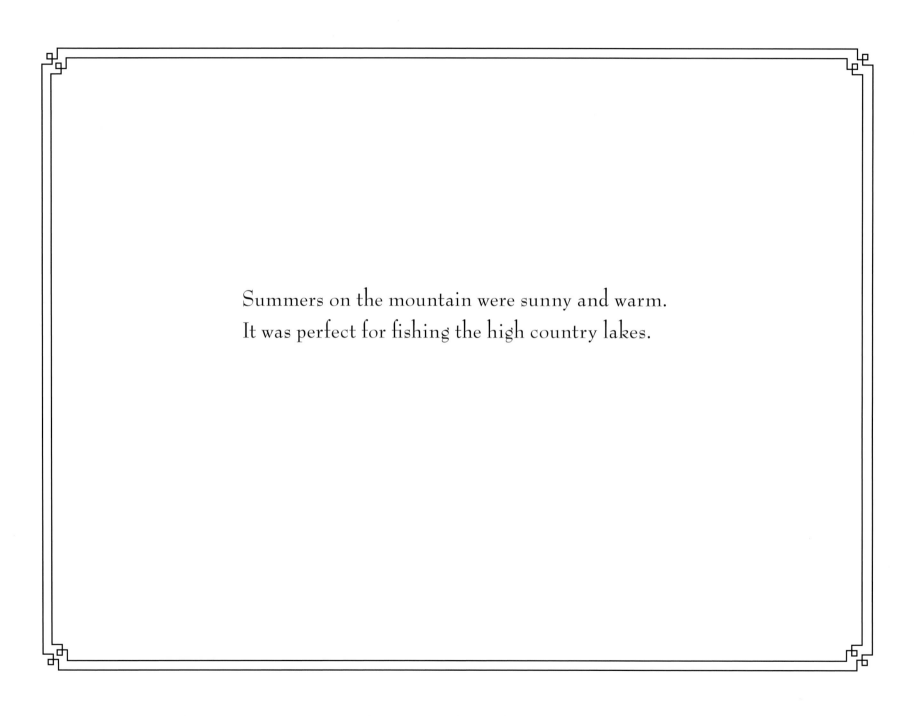

Summers on the mountain were sunny and warm.
It was perfect for fishing the high country lakes.

After a number of years, Billy had grown to be a man and his mountain was changing about as much as he was. Because of the extra rain and snowfall on the highest peaks, a large lake began to form on the east side of the mountain, winding several miles down to Billy's farm. In fact, the shoreline of the new lake ran right next to Billy's house. High above the farm, dozens of magical waterfalls tumbled off the steep cliffs and the forests spread down the mountain onto the prairie. Billy could go fishing and swimming in the new lake or take his canoe to the lake's upper end to go camping and exploring below the towering canyon walls and into the heart of the mountain wilderness.

In the evenings, Billy would sit on the porch overlooking the lake with a few of his neighbors and Old Man Jim. They would talk about fishing and mountain adventures, and what things were like when Kansas was flat.

Many more years passed and Old Man Jim died. Billy had become a husband and father, and shared the mountain with his kids, one of whom he named Jim.

Tall trees, some over 100 feet, covered the mountain as velvety green moss began growing over old dead tree trunks and rocks. Ferns and flowers grew below the dark forest canopy while many varieties of animals moved onto the mountain making it their home. It was beautiful, just like in Billy's childhood book.

When Billy became an old man, he often took hikes or horseback rides up the trails of his mountain with his grandchildren to go fishing and camping or to stay in the family cabin. Billy would often think of Old Man Jim who had helped him with his dream. He remembered all the adventures and magical times the mountain had provided him and his family and friends. Standing next to his favorite fishing hole, watching his grandchildren play on his mountain, Billy realized his dream had truly become a reality. You see, even in Kansas you can have snow-capped mountains if you have dreams you believe in, and even a small boy can move mountains and achieve the impossible.

About the Author

Stephen Richardson grew up in Las Cruces, New Mexico, and graduated from New Mexico State University in 1993, where he studied geography and communications. He then moved to the Grand Canyon in Arizona where he began to develop his photography skills, later making a career in portrait photography. After living briefly in Colorado he has since made Albuquerque his home. His scenic and architectural photography has been published frequently in national scenic calendars, on postcards, and in magazines. Steve started writing children's books in his early 30's after dealing with the deaths of his brother John, his mother, and two nephews who were just children when they died. Writing became his source for meaning and a way to bring purpose to the lives of those who had passed on. His ultimate goal through writing is to make an impact on world poverty and on those who suffer mentally and physically. He has been inspired and influenced by the following people: Gordon Lightfoot, Dan Fogelberg, Judy Collins, John Denver, Miguel Cervantes, Mark Twain, Thomas Jefferson and Ralph Waldo Emerson, among others. He was also inspired by the love and support of his family, and from many friends, including: mother Shirley Dial Richardson and father Albert Richardson; siblings Corinne, Beth, David, Margy, Anne and John; his Uncle Jim and wife Robin; friends Chris and Matt Tegmeyer, Suzanne Dufner, Richard Helbock, Ingrid Truemper, Steve and Shelly Peugh, and John and Anne Mueller.

Thank you all for your love, support, and inspiration. I am truly blessed!

Web site: **www.impossibledreamspub.com**

About the Illustrator

Herb Leonhard was born in Munich, Germany but grew up in the United States. One of his earliest memories was of a beautifully illustrated series of German children's books. This, along with a childhood spent within the pages of comic books, inevitably led to a career as an artist with a love of many of the classic illustrators, both traditional and contemporary, including the Pre-Raphaelites, Maxfield Parrish, Alphonse Mucha, Brian Froud and Roger Dean.

Having been a professional illustrator and graphic designer for more than twenty years, he remains able to observe the natural world around us with a sense of wonder, and sees every subsequent painting and drawing as a new learning experience. His published illustration works include the book "Lyrics" by Tori Amos, "Matthew's Box" by K.B. Reish, a series of classic fairy tales for Glenndoman Korea and his own coloring book, "The Faerie Garden".

He lives in the Pacific Northwest with his wife Allyson, son Laurent, one horse, one dog, two cats and a plethora of chickens.

His work can be seen at **www.herbleonhard.com**

quixotic \kwik-SOT-ik\, *adjective:*

1. Caught up in the romance of noble deeds and the pursuit of unreachable goals; foolishly impractical especially in the pursuit of ideals.

Inspiration

Billy's Mountain was inspired by the works of many artists and writers, however, Miguel Cervantes's novel, Don Quixote de La Mancha (Recently voted the greatest novel ever written) and his "quest" to reach for the impossible dream, had the greatest impact on the author of Billy's Mountain.

Perhaps no group of statesmen enjoyed Don Quixote more than the Founding Fathers of the United States. It was a favorite of Washington, Hamilton, Franklin, Adams (who traveled with the book in his saddlebags), and Thomas Jefferson (who kept several copies of the book in various languages in his library at his home in Monticello, VA). Jefferson often quoted Don Quixote in letters to colleagues and friends, and his writing of the Declaration of Independence and his other impacts on our current "Jeffersonian" democracy are proof that "Quixotic" idealism, which is often made fun of, can profoundly impact the world for the better, taking once thought absurd, unreachable ideas and turning them into a reality so normal they become a regular part of every day life. As Don Quixote said "I come in a world of Iron to make a world of Gold."

Our country was founded on "Quixotic" idealism and, perhaps, that is why we were the first to reach the moon and put spacecraft beyond our solar system. We literally did dream the impossible and reach the unreachable! Makes you wonder what other "absurd" ideas we will see come true in our lifetime?

"Ordinary people believe only in the possible. Extraordinary people visualize not what is possible or probable, but rather what is impossible. And by visualizing the impossible, they begin to see it as possible." - Cherie Carter-Scott

So, if you haven't attempted to tilt a few windmills, or build a snow-capped mountain next to your house, then you don't know what you are missing, or more importantly, what the world might be missing!

Special Thanks to the following people:

Thank you Herb Leonhard for taking Billy's Mountain and bringing it to life with your magical and absolutely stunning illustrations. Thanks to the city and residents of Abilene, Kansas for allowing me to change the landscape of your beautiful area even if it is just in the imaginations of those who read this book. Abilene was the birthplace of my mother, Shirley Dial Richardson, born there in 1927, and it holds a special place in my heart. Special thanks to the following people for their help with editing and suggestions for the book: Albert Richardson (father), Jim Richardson (uncle) and his wife Robin Snagg, Elisabeth Anderson (sister), Sue Beckman (sister-in-law), Ingrid Truemper, Tracie Davis, John Mueller, Anne Mueller, Laura Metzler and Dorothy Williams.

Billy's Mountain Lesson Plan For Teachers

"Teachers are encouraged to discuss Billy's Mountain with an emphasis on making goals (or dreams) and reaching goals (or dreams)." Emphasis is also on getting and accepting help from a trusted new friend." Here are some questions that can be used to guide children with the more complex ideas in the book.

Questions:

Billy's friends didn't think it would be possible to finish the mountain, yet Billy didn't give up. Do you think it was a good idea for Billy to keep trying?

Would you have listened to the criticism (remarks) of your friends?"

Even though Billy needed help building the mountain was he still a good leader?

What makes Billy a good leader?

Could Billy have accomplished the mountain by himself or did he need Old Man Jim's help? Did Jim need help building the mountain? Who helped Old Man Jim and Billy build the mountain?

Building a mountain is an almost impossible task. What are some things from the past that people thought were impossible but turned out not to be impossible?

Teachers can offer these examples if the kids are having trouble:

    a) Mankind sending spacecraft to outer space and walking on the Moon.
    b) Radios
    c) Televisions
    d) Computers
    e) Airplanes and jet propulsion
    f) Cell Phones
    g) iPods
    h) Satellites

What are some things that people think are impossible now but could possibly be invented or accomplished in the future to make the world a better place?

Examples for kids:

    a) Cures for diseases like cancer
    b) Slowing or ending world poverty and hunger
    c) Traveling at the speed of light
    d) Traveling to other solar systems
    e) A device that can read people's thoughts
    f) Ending all wars

Do you have an "impossible dream" that you would like to work on? What dream is that?

How can you make that dream a reality?